My Car by Byron Barton
Mi carro por Byron Barton

Translated from the English by Andrea Montejo

Greenwillow Books, *An Imprint of HarperCollinsPublishers*

My Car / Mi carro. Copyright © 2001 by Byron Barton. Translation by Andrea Montejo. All rights reserved. Manufactured in China. No part of this book may be used or reproduced in any manner whatsoever without written permission except in the case of brief quotations embodied in critical articles and reviews. For information address HarperCollins Children's Books, a division of HarperCollins Publishers, 195 Broadway, New York, NY 10007. www.harpercollinschildrens.com

The full-color art was created in Adobe Photoshop™. The text type is Avant Garde Gothic. First Spanish-English bilingual edition published by Greenwillow Books in 2016

The Library of Congress has cataloged the Greenwillow English-language edition of this title as follows: Barton, Byron. My car / written and illustrated by Byron Barton. p cm. "Greenwillow Books." Summary: Sam describes in loving detail his car and how he drives it. ISBN 978-0-06-245545-1 (bilingual hardback)—ISBN 978-0-06-245544-4 (bilingual pbk.) [1. Automobiles—Fiction.] I. Title. PZ7.B2848 My 2001 [E]—dc21 00-050334
16 17 18 19 20 SCP 10 9 8 7 6 5 4 3 2 1

I am Sam.

Yo soy Sam.

I love my car.
Yo adoro mi carro.

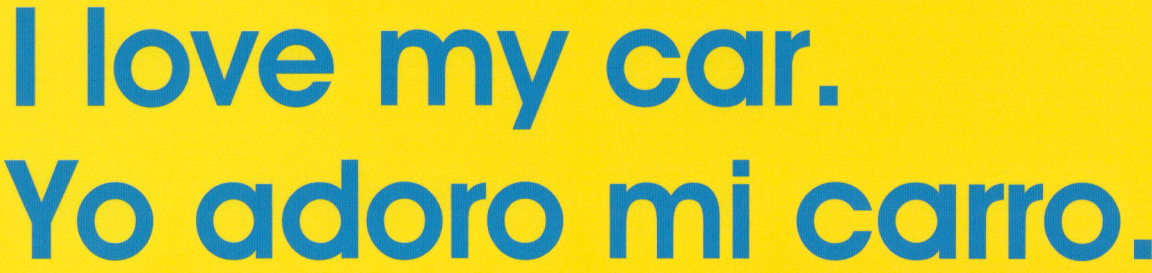

I keep my car clean.
Yo limpio mi carro.

and a full tank of gasoline.

y un tanque lleno de gasolina.

My car has many parts.

Mi carro tiene muchas partes.

My car has lights to see at night

Mi carro tiene luces para ver de noche

Cuando conduzco, conduzco con cuidado.

I obey the laws.

Sigo las reglas.

Doy paso los peatones.

MAIN ST

BUS • BUS

ONE WAY UNA VÍA →

NO PARKING

PROHIBIDO ESTACIONAR

I read the signs.

Leo las señales.

I drive my car
to many places.

Yo conduzco
mi carro para ir
a muchos lugares.

I drive my car to work.

Yo conduzco mi carro para ir al trabajo.

But when
I work,

Pero cuando
trabajo

conduzco mi bus.